Steve Parish™

KIDS

Say
"Hello"
Joey

*Get ready
to jump...*

Joey is going to jump.

Get ready to jump...

...jump right over grasshopper.

We can jump together.

Are you ready?

Jump right over frog.

Frog tells joey he can hop.

Help frog show joey how ...

...to hop right over possum.

Possum says, "Follow me".

Follow possum's footprints ...

...to visit koala at the top of the tree.

"Come and meet my friend," says koala.

Climb this branch ...

...to meet sugar glider in the tree tops.

"Let's say 'Hello' to my neighbour," says sugar glider.

Come on, let's go gliding.

Glide over to meet kookaburra.

Kookaburra loves to fly.

Let him show you how.

Fly over emu's head.

Emu can't fly but emu can run. Can you?

Get ready, go!

Run right up to echidna.

Echidna can't run fast, but he can hide.

Show joey where to hide.

Hide behind scratching wombat.

Wombat can't jump.
Wombat can't hop.
Wombat can't climb, glide or fly.

Wombat can dig!

Dig around joey's sleepy mum.

"Jump into my pouch,"
says Mum.

Show joey where to jump.

Jump inside Mum's pouch.

Joey likes to jump, but after all that hopping, climbing, running, hiding, and digging, he's very tired.

Aren't you?